a novel

THE SECRET LIST

Stephen Palmisano

Order this book online at www.trafford.com
or email orders@trafford.com

Most Trafford titles are also available at major online book retailers.

Printed in Victoria, BC, Canada.

ISBN: 978-1-4269-1598-7 (sc)
ISBN: 978-1-4269-1599-4 (hc)

Library of Congress Control Number: 2009940359

Our mission is to efficiently provide the world's finest, most comprehensive book publishing service, enabling every author to experience success. To find out how to publish your book, your way, and have it available worldwide, visit us online at www.trafford.com

Trafford rev. 02/10/10

 www.trafford.com

North America & international
toll-free: 1 888 232 4444 (USA & Canada)
phone: 250 383 6864 ♦ fax: 812 355 4082

TABLE OF CONTENTS

INTRODUCTION

Adolf Hitler, who was the leader of the National Socialist German Workers party came to power in Germany on January 30, 1933, when the aging president, Paul Von Hindenburg named him to be Chancellor of Germany. Hitler's political party, which was known as the Nazis, was swift to take revenge on their political rivals, and the Jews who he blamed for Germany's economic troubles. Hitler's political enemies, the Jews, and the Gypsies were in for a rough time, first in Germany, and then in each country where the Nazis came to power. No one could imagine the ruthlessness that awaited these different groups, or the genocide that followed.

This novel deals with the hardships, and life altering decisions, that had to be made by a Jewish family living in Vienna, Austria, who found themselves trapped in their country by the swift Nazi takeover. The different plans and schemes by the family member in their effort to leave Austria, and to escape the jurisdiction of the Nazis are attempted along with the unexpected opportunities that life brings to all. Part of their plan was to hide their one year old grandson in a Catholic convent orphanage to keep him safe, so that he could survive the Nazis final solution intended for all Jews. Finally at the end of the war, the difficulty that the family members who survived, had in re-claiming their grandson from the Catholic Church, who resisted the return of the Jewish children placed in their care.

CHAPTER I

Political Storm Clouds

The weather on the first day of spring of 1936 in Vienna was beautiful. The promise of renewal that spring brings each year usually lifts the spirits of even the staunchest pessimist. This would be true here in Vienna, if not for the hard times of the worlds economic depression. Things were tough for most in Austria, except the fortunate few. The rise of Hitler to power in Germany, and the recent political troubles in our homeland was very upsetting, especially for our small Jewish minority. Political storm clouds over Europe seemed on a collision course that couldn't be stopped. This started in March of 1933, when Chancellor Engelbert Dollfuss of Austria adjourned Parliament. This act was sure to cause trouble between the Christian Socialist Party and the opposition Social Democratic Party. Sure enough, a political war between the two parties resulted, and although short lived, divided the loyalties of the citizens. The Christian Socialist's were against uniting Austria and Germany. The Social Democrats and the local Nazi party wanted this unity. Although Dollfuss ruled as a dictator, his rule was short lived. He was soon assassinated, it was rumored, by the Nazis. Dollfuss was succeeded by Kurt Von Schuschnigg as Chancellor. He too wanted to keep Austria independent from Germany. Austria was mostly Roman Catholic, and our small Jewish community coexisted peacefully with them, but not with the pro Nazis. It was in this atmosphere of 1936 that the Jewish community had to exist.

Our recently married daughter, Sara and her husband Ari, phoned us early that spring morning to invite us to their small apartment home for Passover Seder. Ari's grandparents, parents, and younger sister would also be there. This would be Sara's first hosting of a Passover Seder. She was very excited, as my wife told me after her phone call. My name is Jacob Silver. My wife Rebecca and I have always lived in Vienna. I am a History Teacher in a nearby elementary school. My wife works in the local library. Both of us are in our early fifties and have no thought of retirement. Our only child Sara, has been married for almost a year. We anxiously hope that soon we will be told that a grandchild is on the way, but so far nothing has been said. Sara's husband, Ari Fenerman, is a ski instructor at a nearby ski resort. This is where he met our Sara, who had sought ski lessons. The courtship was swift, and soon she was getting free lessons from her new husband.

As the first days of spring passed, the start of the Passover celebration would soon be here. The Seder dinner being hosted by Sara, was on the following weekend. Sara was in constant communication with her mother to make sure she got everything right. She wanted to make a good impression on Ari's parents and grandparents. The day for our daughter's first Seder arrived, and that morning was spent by my wife answering numerous phone calls from Sara requesting guidance. We arrived at our daughter's home with my wife's contributions to the dinner in plenty of time for her to help Sara with the preparations.

The other guests had not yet arrived, so Ari and I took this opportunity to talk about the current political events troubling our country. Soon the other guests arrived, and we all exchanged our salutations and blessings on this celebration of Passover. Ari's parents were in their early forties, and his grandparents were in their sixties. His younger sister, his only sibling, was just twelve years old. She was twelve years younger than Ari, who was twenty four years old. Our daughter Sara was twenty two years old.

The Passover Seder went very smoothly and I could see the glee in Sara's eyes on her successful hosting of the event. Ari's grandfather led us in the torah readings that are part of the tradition for Passover. After the final toasting of the Seder meal, all of us men adjourned to the parlor, while the ladies took care of the cleanup. Ari's father Joseph, soon brought up the topic of the political turmoil that was going on, and told us that he and his wife Brenda and their daughter Rachael, were thinking of leaving Austria with Ari's grandparents, if the situation became any more hazardous for the Jews. They urged Ari to also consider the move, but he thought that his father was over reacting. Besides, he said, Sara and I have an announcement to share with all of you. This peaked everyone's curiosity, and Sara was summoned from the kitchen with the other ladies to announce her pregnancy. Ari's grandmother, Golda exclaimed to Ari's mother Brenda; "See, I told you she looked pregnant."

Ari's grandparents, Simon Fenerman and his wife Golda had another son, Joshua. He lived in New York City with his family. Joshua urged them, and all the other family members to immigrate to America. He was successful in business, and had the means to sponsor all that would decide to come. Ari's father was considering this move, but Ari was opposed to leaving Austria. His love for skiing, and the beautiful Austrian Alps was something that he dreaded leaving. Simon and Golda said they were too old to wait for the political troubles to end, and had made up their minds. They urged Joseph and Brenda to seriously consider the move for their families safety. That evening after all the traditional practices for Passover had been fulfilled, we parted company, and returned to our small home with the good news of the coming birth of our first grandchild and the depressing news topics of conversation that occurred that day about the turmoil that engulfed our nation.

The weather in Vienna in the summer of 1936 was very pleasant. As the days of summer passed by, Sara's baby bump was growing visibly larger. The news coming out of Germany was not so pleasant. The refugees coming from Germany, to escape the Nazi terror, brought this news. For those of us that would be affected by a Nazi takeover here in Austria, this news was very upsetting.

Sara's baby was due to enter the world before he start of the Chanukah season. Her pregnancy went smoothly, and her husband seemed more excited about the coming event than Sara did. It was late November on the 26th of 1936 when their son was born. They chose the name Jonathan for their new son. At his circumcision by the Rabbi at temple, both Rebecca and I, along with Ari's parents, sister, and grandparents were there. My wife decided to host a Chanukah celebration that was due to arrive in the coming weeks. It started to seem to me that Ari's grandparents had chosen wisely in their decision to immigrate to America. When my wife phoned Ari's parents to invite them for Chanukah, they told her that they had also decided to go to America. Ari's grandparents, Simon and Golda, his parents, Joseph and Brenda, and his sister Rachael, were all to leave Austria at the end of Chanukah, at the years end. This Chanukah celebration would also be a farewell gathering for our son-in-law's loved ones.

CHAPTER II

Our New Grandson

Our new grandson Jonathan, was a strong and healthy baby. He had a continuous smile on his face. Rebecca and I thought he was truly adorable. His light complexion, blue eyes, and dark hair, although scarce, gave a very striking appearance. Sara and Ari seemed to be delighted with their chores of taking care of Jonathan. If the political turmoil of the times wasn't a factor, their outlook would be very happy.

Chanukah arrived and our gathering was to occur on the eighth day of the celebration. Although our home was small, and our financial resources limited, we went all out to provide the best of everything for our guests. The soon departure of Ari's family to America was very sad for him, but knowing that they would be out of harms way was also comforting to him. The uncertainty of our future, for those of us remaining in Austria, was very troubling. There were ugly rumors coming out of Germany about the terrible things that the Jewish community was enduring. No official news, but we were all convinced that the rumors were true. Simon and Joseph had visas from the American Embassy for their family's immigration. Their route would take them by rail from Vienna, through the danger of Mussolini's Italy, to the port city of Genoa. Hopefully their American visas would protect them from any harassment by the Fascists. There they would all board a ship to travel through the Mediterranean Sea, across the Atlantic Ocean, to America. When Ari received a cable from his father that they were all safe at his uncle's in New York City, he was relieved of the worries of their traveling through Italy.

So much for their troubles, now we that remained in Austria must make plans for our escape if the Nazis took over, as seemed to be what was happening. After the ski season ended with the approach of Spring and Summer of 1937, Ari could spend more time at home with Sara and his new son. He could be there to experience his son's development. Watching Jonathan scurry across the room on his hands and knees, and then taking his first steps was very pleasant. Soon Jonathan was starting to form words. Ari and Sara seemed very happy.

The weather in the summer of 1937 was ideal. Vienna was in her glory, just like a beautiful lady at a fancy ball. The days seemed to come and go very fast, as they always do in summer. I suppose this is true everywhere, as no one desires the approach of fall and winter. It was on one of these beautiful summer days that Rebecca and I asked Sara and Ari to take a walk in the park. My teaching duties were over for the summer recess, and Rebecca was also on vacation from her job at the library. We all met at the park, and then stopped at a nearby cafe for a light lunch. After lunch we all resumed our stroll. Sara and Ari, with Jonathan in a stroller, walked ahead and Rebecca and I followed. As we walked along the path, we were met by two Catholic nuns approaching us from the opposite direction. As the older of the two nuns got near to us, both she and my wife broke out into gleeful exuberance. After the hugs and salutations, Rebecca explained to us that she and this nun, now Sister Margaret, were childhood neighbors and best friends. The difference in their religious beliefs never interfered with their close friendship.

Rebecca then introduced me, Sara, Ari, and little Jonathan, to her old friend. Sister Margaret then insisted that Rebecca and I come to her convent on the following day, and said it was most important that we do so. We were given the directions and time for this meeting, and again the importance of this meeting was emphasized. Sister Margaret and Rebecca then exchanged hugs again and we parted company. For the rest of our walk in the park that afternoon, I couldn't get this strange unexpected meeting out of my mind.

At the appointed time on the following day, we arrived at Sister Margaret's convent. It was then that we found out that she was the Mother Superior. She was in charge of the convent and all the functions that were part of the convent complex, including the orphanage, and the old age home. We both were brought to Sister Margaret's office by a young nun, and it was obvious that we were expected. Sister Margaret greeted us warmly, and told us she was happy that we didn't change our minds about this visit. She then said that we should accompany her to her private outside garden, where we could talk in private. After she showed us the beautiful flowers and features of the garden, we all sat on a stone bench for our talk.

She told Rebecca that the rumors she was sure that we had heard about the terrible things that were happening to the Jews in Germany had been verified by the clergy that were coming to Austria from Germany. She told us that it was the Nazis intention to annex Austria, and that we should leave as soon as possible with our daughter and her family.

"If this isn't possible and you get stranded here, I want you to know that I will be here for you as much as I can. You're grandson can be hidden in our orphanage for as long as needed, and issued forged documents to hide his Jewish background, if you find this necessary. If both of you need my help, I will hide you in the convent, and try and help you leave the country. Both of you can be disguised, and furnished forged identity documents, and travel with a group of clergy to Italy. From Italy, I can arrange for your escape to Switzerland. Please don't take this warning lightly."

Sister Margaret then brought us to a parlor where tea and cookies were served. With tears in their eyes, Sister Margaret and Rebecca bid each other farewell. We then were escorted out of the convent. This meeting was very upsetting to both of us, and we felt an urgency to discuss this with Sara and Ari. On the way home I commented to Rebecca, that you and Sister Margaret must have been very close friends when you were children. She responded with four words, "The best of friends." That evening we went to Sara's apartment to discuss that afternoons meeting with Rebecca's old friend. After explaining to both Sara and Ari, the urgent warning that Sister Margaret had given to us, their attitude seemed to be that we were overreacting. Ari pointed out that our chancellor and his Christian Socialist Party, who were in control in Austria, were opposed to unification with Germany. Ari with bravado in his manner, then said he could get to Switzerland at any time he wished with his knowledge of the passes through the mountains and the ski trails that he knew about. "That's fine for you." I said, "but what about Sara and Jonathan?". He responded that Sara was also a good skier and with his help, he was sure that they wouldn't have any difficulty. "What about Jonathan?" I repeated, "Could he also ski across the mountains?" This comment subdued his bravado on his ability to escape if the Nazis took control. Rebecca then told Sara and Ari of the offers of help from her friend, Sister Margaret.

After our visit, I was sure that our children would at least now think seriously about about the need to leave Austria, if this terrible threatening Nazi takeover of our country came to pass.

The political climate in Austria in the summer of 1937 was beginning to show the results of fear and intimidation. More and more, the people were afraid to voice their opposition to the unification with Germany. It became apparent to the Jewish community, that if and when there was a Nazi takeover, there would be few to raise their voice in opposition. Those few brave individuals who spoke against the Nazis were soon silenced permanently. It was now difficult to find any Austrian to openly voice their opposition to unification with Germany.

CHAPTER III

The Rabbi's Warning

That weekend at Temple, it was noticeable that there were fewer in attendance. Our Rabbi, who was usually very jovial, seemed quite solemn. In his sermon he explained the reason for the light attendance that he was sure that we had noticed. Then in alphabetical order he named the families that have left Austria to escape the eminent threat of a Nazi takeover. "This summer of 1937 was the start of a new exodus for our Jewish brethren," he said. He then went on to tell us the latest information that he heard of, about the treatment of Jews in Germany. Rabbi told how the Nazis had stationed German troops in the Rhineland with disregard for the treaty that prohibited this act with no action by the allied nations. He wondered how long it would be before Hitler marched on Austria. He recommended that all of us that could, leave Austria for a safer location, and do so as soon as possible. After Temple that day, the unusual amount of hugs and friendly demeanor among our group indicated the extent of fear and worry that we all felt.

In the following weeks we received word of the many families that were disposing of their possessions at ridiculous low prices. This apparently in preparation for a quick move. "How sad," I said to Rebecca. "You labor for a lifetime to accumulate things to pass down to your children, and then you have to discard them for an escape to safety." We never were wealthy enough to be able to have valuable things, but we did have those items which were dear to us, and those mementos that were reminders of our long time together.

Both Rebecca and I then seemed to take careful stock of all our possessions, to see what we would leave, and what we would like to take with us if we had to leave Austria quickly. Surprisingly there was very little that we had that was important to us, except for our wedding rings, some photographs, and some legal documents. I know that my wife had many discussions with our daughter on this same topic.

Summer passed too quickly in this worri-some atmosphere, and the fall season ushered in with first, the beautiful colors of the vegeta-tion that were everywhere, and then the first snowfall that meant the start of the ski season. Ari, of course, was delighted with the return of his job as a ski instructor, and the busy activity at the resort where he was employed. Jonathan's first birthday was coming soon, and my wife and daughter were absorbed with preparations for a party to be at our Sara's apartment. Ari's parents were all in America now, so we were the only family to be at this birthday celebration. November 26, 1937 arrived, and Rebecca very carefully wrapped our birthday gifts. She also made a potato salad and one of her favorite vegetable casseroles to bring to the party. We arrived at Sara's apartment just after the noon hour. She was busily putting the finishing touches to the birthday cake. She was so proud of her success at the first cake for her baby. Shortly after we arrived, Ari came home accompanied by a close friend who was a coworker at the ski resort. Introductions were given by Ari. His name was Adam Mendorer. He appeared to be approximately the same age as Ari, and worked in the ski resort sporting goods shop. He was Jewish, as was evident by his yamica.

It was nice to have an added guest for the birthday party. Ari then told us that Adam's girlfriend was also coming to the party, and she would be there soon. After a short time, Adam's girlfriend arrived. She was a young Jewish girl that had left Germany when Hitler became Chancellor. Her name was Gretchen Goldberg. She was a very pretty girl with a pleasant smile. Sara and Rebecca set the dinner table, and soon we all sat down to this very joyful birthday dinner party. After dinner and the table was cleared, Sara brought out the birthday cake. We all complimented her on her beautiful baking job. Jonathan seemed delighted with the cake, and even blew out the birthday candles with some help and guidance from Ari. After the cake was served, the gifts were brought out and given to Jonathan. He made short work of the meticulously wrapped gifts. The gifts were mostly clothes and practical things, then Ari brought out the musical top. Jonathan was laughing and giggling as Ari showed how it worked. After this wonderful dinner party, Rebecca and Gretchen helped Sara with the cleanup, while Ari, his friend Adam, and I, played with Jonathan and talked of the recent news. I asked Adam if his parents lived in Vienna. He told me that they had immigrated to England with his siblings. I asked why he didn't go with them. "I'm in love with Gretchen" was his response. He couldn't leave Austria without her. Adam then went on to tell us of the difficult time she had in leaving Germany. Her parents and grandparents are in a concentration camp in Germany. She will not leave Austria until she hears some news about them. Adam then told us of the terrible things that were happening to the Jews since the Nazi takeover in Germany. "The things that Gretchen had told me are very upsetting," he told us. He then said that if the Nazis come to Austria, we must leave as quickly as possible. On the way home I related this conversation to Rebecca, and asked her to try to convince Sara and Ari to leave Austria with their son, and join Ari's parents in America.

The eight days of Chanukah would soon be here, but the level of preparations at Temple were very subdued. On the Sabbath, the Rabbi explained that many of our temples sacred artifacts had been sent to Switzerland and then on to England with some of our brethren who had already left Austria. This, he said, was for their safekeeping. He then glanced over to our temple's large Menorah, and said that we will keep our Menorah until after our Chanukah celebration. This too will then be sent out of the country for its safekeeping. I know that we all pray that we, along with our sacred artifacts, can be reunited, hopefully in our true homeland. Our numbers at temple, again, seemed fewer than our last meeting. When the days of Chanukah arrived, our celebrations at temple seemed less enthusiastic, and again with fewer brethren.

Rebecca's pleading's with our daughter and her husband, to consider leaving the country, went in one ear and out the other. I also told Ari of our Rabbi's warnings, but to no avail. Rebecca wouldn't consider leaving Austria without our children also leaving. All I could do is wait for the inevitable to happen.

CHAPTER IV

The Nazi Takeover

It was March, 1938 when Hitler unilaterally claimed that Germany and Austria were one unified nation. The news spread like wild fire throughout Vienna. The Christian Socialist Party leaders were in a hurry to leave Austria before the arrival of the German troops. They too, along with the Jews, would end up in concentration camps, for being opposed to unification with Germany. All of a sudden, everyone said they were for unification, but I suspect that this was out of fear. Even though, in our hearts, we all knew it would happen, it still came as a shock. Everyone who felt threatened were now in a mindless rush to dispose of their property and belongings that couldn't be taken with them in their flight from their homeland. They all knew they must leave Austria before the Nazi troops arrived to close the borders. The abandonment of their property in their rush to leave was a heartbreaking scene. To watch those in panic go through this while others who also should leave Austria, but couldn't believe in the cruelty of the rumors, just stood their ground to see what would happen. I heard one old gentleman at Temple say, "After all, they can't kill all of us."

Rebecca and I sorted through our belongings, and we each kept only what could fit into a knapsack, in preparation for a quick exit from Austria. Each of us took what we needed for our survival, and those things that were most dear to us. We had decided that Switzerland would be our destination for refuge from the Nazis. We both decided   not to dispose of any of our belongings, and to leave everything behind rather than mimic what others in their panic to leave were doing.

Rebecca proceeded to clean our house, and to put everything in it's proper place. I asked her why she was doing this? Her response was that whoever takes our home shouldn't think that we were unkept. On leaving our home we couldn't decide if we should lock the door. I said that if we lock the door, someone would probably break it down to get in. If we don't lock it, it would provide a clue to when we left, which is not good if the Nazis are looking for us. Rebecca asked if we should say goodbye to our neighbors. "I don't think thats a good idea," I answered. We decided to lock the door and leave the key under the door mat. We both took a long look around, and Rebecca said "shalom" in a low voice, and I repeated her words.

We had one last chance to try to convince Sara and Ari to leave Austria. We went directly to their apartment. Sara was home alone with Jonathan. She responded to our pleading by telling us that she would do whatever her husband decided to do. We told Sara that we left our home and were going to seek political asylum in Switzerland. While we were discussing this, Ari came home. He told us that the news was everywhere that the Nazi troops arrived and closed the borders. Our plans to escape to Switzerland were too late. We talked about all of our situations, and we all agreed that Rebecca's friend, Sister Margaret's offer was the best option for Rebecca and I, and our grandson Jonathan. Rebecca called Sister Margaret on the telephone, and made arrangements to go to her convent that next evening. We stayed at our children's apartment that night. The next morning was very solemn as Sara and Ari packed some things for Jonathan's stay at the convent orphanage.

The day seemed to fly by so swiftly, and that evening at dinner, which was to be our last meal with our children was very emotional for all. After dinner we started on the long walk to the convent. This hour long walk was done so that we wouldn't jeopardize our benefactors by having witnesses to our being there. When we arrived at the convent, and stood by the door, the reality hit me that after this meeting, we no longer would all be together.

We rang the doorbell and Sister Lucille came to the door. She was the same young nun that answered the door at our previous meeting. It was apparent that we were expected, and were quickly let in, and escorted to Sister Margaret's office. Sister Margaret greeted us warmly and it was reassuring to us to be received so kindly. After discussing our situation with her, and telling her of our decision to have Jonathan stay in the convent orphanage, as she had previously suggested, and also to conceal Rebecca and me in the convent until our escape to Switzer-land could be arranged. Sara and Ari still intended to leave Austria by going over the mountains to Switzerland. We hopefully would all be reunited there. It was heartbreaking to see Jonathan leaving the arms of Sara and Ari, to be hidden in the orphanage, but we all knew it was necessary. His name would be changed to John Wickischer, a very Christian Austrian name, we were all told. Remember this for future reference. All his papers and birth certificate would indicate that he was left by our convent door as a newborn on November 26, 1936. Rebecca and I would be given forged identity documents, and work in the convent old age home kitchen until we could escape to Switzerland.

Sister Margaret asked Sister Lucille to take Jonathan to the orphanage. It was sad to see this separation of mother and father from their child. When Sister Lucille took Jonathan into her arms from Sara, our daughter started to cry, and Ari who was trying to console her, also had tears. This was the first time I saw my son-in-law cry, and it was probably a rare experience for him. Sister Margaret then said to Rebecca that she would give us a moment alone to say our farewells. With that, she left us alone in the office. We all hugged one another, and I wondered how long it would be before we were reunited. Ari then told us that he, Sara, his friend Adam, Adam's girlfriend Gretchen, would all cross the mountains into Switzerland. They had their clothes, equipment, and backpacks ready for this venture. He was confident of success. With this we bid our goodbyes and gave our blessings.

"Shalom", we all repeated. Sister Margaret then came back, and called for another nun to escort Sara and Ari to the door. Sister Margaret and Rebecca then reflected on their happy days of their childhood. Sister Margaret told us not to worry about Jonathan, and that he would be well taken care of in the convent orphanage. We both were then taken to the convent old age home, and shown to our living quarters.

CHAPTER V

Our Stay At The Convent

We were given a small room in an area adjacent to the old age section of the convent, dedicated for lay workers. We had a small combination bedroom, living room, kitchenette, and bathroom. The identity papers provided by Sister Margaret gave us the cover names of Hans and Greta Gruber. Our ages on the forged documents were approximately the same as our real ages. Our work duties were varied. Kitchen work, cleaning, and laundry, but for the most part, we took care of the needs of the elderly residents who were too old or infirm to care for themselves. We were not allowed to go to the convent orphanage to see Jonathan, as this could endanger both him and the other Jewish refugee babies hidden there. Sister Margaret was very firm on this point in spite of the pleading by Rebecca.

Spring passed, and summer, which usually goes by so quickly, seemed to go by very slowly. I guess this was because we were so anxious to get our permission to make our escape to Switzerland. There was a visit to the convent old age home by the German Gestapo to check everyones identity papers. This inspection seemed to go without any problem, except that I did notice that one of the Gestapo inspectors write something in his notebook when checking each resident of the oldage home. This seemed strange to me. Later, when I mentioned this to Rebecca, she told me that Sister Margaret told her in one of their meetings that there were rumors coming from Germany, that the Nazis were practicing euthanasia. Disgusting, I thought. I wonder what lay ahead for the residents of our home. Finally, the fall of 1938 arrived. I wondered when and if we would ever be given the word that it was time to escape from Austria to Switzerland. Fall passed without our being able to celebrate our grandson's two year birthday. As winter came, the convents population was absorbed with their preparations for the Christmas holiday. Rebecca and I would celebrate Chanukah very discreetly in the privacy of our room. The New Year holiday of 1939 came and passed without much notice at the convent. Again, Rebecca and I celebrated in our room with a little wine provided by Sister Margaret, procured from the convent chapel. We had no news from Sara or Ari, and although we knew that we wouldn't hear from them, you find yourself expecting the impossible.

Winter ended and the spring of 1939 came. Rebecca, after one of her discreet meetings with Sister Margaret, brought me some books to study. She told my wife that I would be disguised as a Catholic Priest during our escape. It would be important for me to be informed about the religion so that I wouldn't expose my disguise. I was instructed to study these books thoroughly so that I wouldn't endanger my companions or the convent. I may even be called upon to perform some priestly duties.

Spring ended and I wondered how long it would be before we could leave. Finally, the word came from Sister Margaret that we would leave the convent on the following week. Rebecca brought two packages from Sister Margaret, which contained outfits for our escape. One outfit was for a nun and the other for a priest. We were also given small canvas bags which contained all of the accessories needed to complete our disguise. We were not to bring along any items from our past as this would endanger everyone.

I must be clean shaven, no beard. Our new identity papers would give our new names as Sister Mary and Father Joseph. "Goodbye to Hans and Greta Gruber" I said aloud, as I looked through these new identity documents. This brought a smile to Rebecca's face.

The Sunday night before our departure, Sister Margaret came to our small apartment. I think that this was actually the first time that she did this. She usually sent someone to summon Rebecca to her office. This was done to minimize our personal contact, so that the close relationship between her and Rebecca was not known by everyone. Sister Magaret was very careful that only a select few of the other nuns knew of our true identity. In these dangerous times it was necessary to be very careful. She asked me if I had studied the books that she had sent to me. I smiled and said that I would say the Catholic Mass for her and give her Communion if she liked. This brought a smile to her face which was so stern when she first came to our apartment. She told me that it would not be necessary. The moment of humor was a pleasant repose to the tense atmosphere. She told us that Sister Lucille would accompany us all the way to Switzerland, as it was customary for nuns to only travel in pairs. "The three of you will travel with another group of nuns from our order who are returning to Italy from their visit here. Once they return to their home convent in Italy, the three of you will leave the others in Italy and follow the route to Switzerland that I have given to Sister Lucille. You must be ready by 5:00 A.M. in the morning.

That is when Sister Lucille will come for you." "One other thing Jacob Silver" she emphasized to me, "I am giving you a secret list which you must guard with your life.

On this list are eight names of the Jewish children in our orphanage. Their real Jewish names, ages, and birth dates, with their new false identities are listed. Hopefully, one day they can be reunited with their families. She then told me that if I am caught by the Nazis, I must make sure that I destroy this list as my first priority. I looked at the eight names on the list. There amongst the others, I found myself staring at my grandson's name, Jonathan Fenerman, born on November 26, 1936, with his new false identity name, John Wickischer, along with the names of four other boys and three girls. Their real names, false names, and birth dates were also listed. The list was on very thin paper for ease in swallowing, if it become necessary.

Sister Margaret gave Rebecca a farewell hug as we would not see her again before we were to leave in the morning. They both were crying as we bid our farewells. She wished us good luck on our trip, with God's blessing. As she left our apartment, we all said in unison, our Jewish salutation, shalom.

CHAPTER VI

Escape To Switzerland

We set the alarm on our clock for 3:30 a.m. And both of us got some sleep for the new adventure that awaited us. By 5:00 a.m. we were both ready and waiting. With measured punctuality, Sister Lucille came for us. With our small canvas bags and our lunch for the trip, we left the protection of the convent in the company of the group of nuns we were traveling with. There were ten other nuns that would be our traveling companions. The original plan was that all of these nuns were to stay in their convent in Italy, but new instructions had just arrived, and six of these nuns would go all the way to Switzerland with us. A small bus was waiting in front of the convent entrance to pick us up for the trip to the rail station. Our train was to depart Vienna at 6:30 a.m. This bus ride to the rail station would be the first time that Rebecca and I had left the protection of the convent since we had first sought sanctuary. The weather was rainy and cloudy and matched the disposition of our group. Our bus ride through the streets of Vienna was to be our last look at our city for a very long time. As I looked out the bus window it seemed that the once happy atmosphere of Vienna now matched the gloomy weather since the Nazi takeover. When we arrived at the rail station and departed the bus, Sister Lucille gave Rebecca and I a biscuit and some tea from a thermos while we waited for the call to board the train. Soon, a uniformed Nazi came by and checked all of our groups identity papers and travel permits. Our disguise worked perfectly and we boarded the train without incident. Our route by rail took us south from Vienna to the cities of Eisenstadt and Kapfenberg, then west to the Bischofshofen and Innsbruck. At Innsbruck the train stopped and let the passengers depart the train for a short time, to let us stretch our legs, eat lunch, and refresh ourselves. Again all passengers had their identity papers and travel permits checked by the Nazis. We then returned to the train to continue our trip. The route then went south through Austria to the Brenner Pass and the border with Italy. At the border we again were asked for our identity papers and travel permits by both the German and the Italian border guards. We passed through without a second glance by anyone. The Italian nuns traveling with us did however give us some strange looks during the course of our trip. The first Italian city on our route was Vipiteno, then we passed through Bressanone, and we all departed the train at the next stop, which was the city of Bulzano. At Bulzano, we were met by a small bus and two other nuns from their order. We were all driven to their convent where supper and overnight accommodations would be provided. For four of the nuns, this was there final destination and they wouldn't be going any further with us. That next morning after mass and breakfast we left the convent in the same bus that had picked us up at the train station. Our traveling party now reduced by four proceeded on to our next destination. The trip from Bulzano by bus on narrow roads brought us to a small town called

Tirano, which was near the border of Switzerland. We stopped there to have lunch and refreshen ourselves at a small parish church convent on the outskirts of the town.

We were just finishing our lunch when a young girl came to the church looking for the parish priest. The priest was off somewhere in the parish and could not be quickly located. I was the only priest available at the church. The girl's mother had sent her for the priest because the young girl's grandfather was dying and wanted the sacrament of the last rites of the church. I, being the only priest that was available, was asked to take the place of the parish priest, and go to this dying man's bedside. I had no idea what to do, however I didn't want to give away my deception of not being a priest. I asked Sister Lucille in German, what was the procedure for giving the last rites. I didn't recall reading about these when Sister Margaret gave me the books to study. Sister Lucille provided a quick course in this with step by step instructions. It was fortunate that none of these locals understood German. I could see that Sister Lucille was very upset in this deception that I was about to start. All through the incident, Sister Lucille nervously repeated the sign of the cross as penitence for her part in this deception. Just as I was about to begin, the parish priest arrived at the bedside of this dying man. The parish priest then gave the last rites to this man. The look of relief on Sister Lucille's face was very evident that she didn't have to participate in my deception. I whispered to Rebecca that I could have performed this ceremony without any problem. She whispered back that I better not get so cocky.

After this incident our group proceeded to the border crossing, and without incident we entered Switzerland. After some brief questioning by the Swiss border guards, we continued on our road trip to St. Moritz where we went directly to the convent which was the destination of our six Italian nuns traveling with us. Sister Lucille would remain at this convent until some group of nuns was to return to Austria. Rebecca and I were given some lay clothes by Sister Lucille, and told to change our outfits away from the convent and the other nuns. We were also told to dispose of our clergy outfits so that the church wasn't implicated in our border crossing deception. We bid farewell to Sister Lucille and sought out a government building where we could request political asylum. After some questioning by the authorities, who took our correct names and nationality and reason for our leaving Austria, we were given asylum. We were careful not to implicate any of our benefactors. We were then driven to an internment camp for refugees. All we had were the clothes on our backs. The few mementos that we had when we left our home in Vienna had to be discarded when we left the convent in Vienna on the orders of Sister Margaret because of the danger it would pose to all of us if they were discovered by the Nazis. The one possession that I did have was the secret list of names of the Jewish children at the convent orphanage in Austria. This I would guard with my life.

CHAPTER VII

The Internment Camp

The camp was much larger than we expected. We were taken to the camp directors office building, and again we were told to fill out a questionnaire documenting our names, nationality, previous country of residence, and the reason we sought asylum. After this check in processing we were both given identity cards. The camp was like a large military barracks complex. Some small cabins reserved for families, that is mother and father with children and old parents. But, for the most part, males were separated from females with each having their own dormitory buildings. This is where Rebecca and I would end up. We each were issued a blanket, a kit for our personal hygiene, and a metal kit for our meals.

There were forty small cabins for family groups, and twenty each of male and female dormitory buildings. All buildings were laid out in a very simple pattern of a single road with buildings on both sides of the road. These roads then interconnected to the camp directors office and buildings used for food preparation, medical clinic, and storage buildings. Most of the residents of this camp were Italians seeking sanctuary from Mussolini's Fascists, and Austrians on the run from the Nazis.

The weather in the summer of 1939 was very pleasant in Switzerland, and after we accustomed ourselves to our new surroundings, both of us wondered what we could now do to locate our daughter Sara and her husband Ari. In the weeks that followed, Rebecca and I would ask every resident of the camp if they knew or heard of either Ari or Sara Fenerman, Adam Mendorer, or Gretchen Goldberg.

No one in this internment camp had any knowledge of any of them. The camp residents were not allowed to leave without permission from the camp director, and there was little chance of getting this without good reason. The Swiss camp director suggested that we ask the Red Cross workers to make inquiries about our children and their friends when they visit the other internment camps. He also told us that the Red Cross headquarters in Geneva has an office that searches for missing persons. The visiting Red Cross workers would give us forms to fill out for this search.

Finally, just before the end of August 1939, the Red Cross arrived at our camp. They brought supplies of many things needed by the camp residents to make their existence more comfortable, including food items not normally provided by the camp and medicine for our personal use. In their company was a nurse who checked the sick. Rebecca and I, thank God, have remained in good health throughout this ordeal. None of the Red Cross workers had heard of our missing children, but they did give us the missing persons report to fill out, with assurance that they would give it to the proper persons in Geneva. This gave Rebecca and I some satisfaction.

September 1939 brought the invasion of Poland by the Nazis and the Russians. This was sure to be the start of World War II. We all wondered if the Germans would also invade Switzerland, but thank God, this didn't happen. If the Germans did come, we would stand little chance of survival. News of what was happening in the war was scarce, and only the occasional visitors and the Red Cross workers brought any news of what was happening. It was on one of these visits that we heard of France and England declaring war on Germany.

Sometime later, we were told of the swift defeat of France and England on the European mainland, and the exodus of the British and French troops at Dunkirk. This was followed by the news of Italy declaring war on France and England on the side of Germany. These were very dark days for all of us at the camp. So far the only news of the war that we received was bad news. We all wondered what would become of us if Germany was to win the war.

Our routine at camp was much the same each day. In the morning all the internees would assemble at the mess hall, and line up with our metal kits for our breakfast. The lines to get food were very long, but Rebecca and I would wait for each other so that we could eat together. Only two meals were served each day, breakfast and dinner. After breakfast, all the abled residents of the camp would go to their assigned work place. Some would be assigned to kitchen duty, others to camp maintenance jobs and general labor for other things necessary to keep the camp functioning smoothly. No one complained about this work, and in fact we were glad to do something constructive to lesson the expense for our Swiss benefactors. Everyone was grateful to the Swiss for this sanctuary.

Each day when Rebecca and I ate our meals together, we would talk about our grandson Jonathan and our daughter Sara and her husband Ari, and wonder about their safety and well being. Not knowing anything about them was very upsetting, but we prayed that they all would be safe, and that we ultimately would be reunited.

Then one day we were summoned to the camp directors office and given a letter from Geneva. Our inquiry had finally been successful. Our search for our children and their friends had located a young man named Adam Mendorer. Adams response to the missing persons inquiry looking for Ari and Sara Fenerman, Gretchen Goldberg, and himself, brought the news that we dreaded to hear. They both were killed by the Nazi border patrol guards in their attempt to flee Austria. No other details were given to us in this letter, but we were told at which internment camp Adam was stationed. Rebecca and I were both devastated by this terrible news, and we both vowed to search him out and be given a more detailed account of our children's death. We also felt the need to somehow inform Ari's parents of this terrible news. Communication from the internment camp with the outside world during these early days of the war was very difficult, and the only hope of contacting anyone was through the Red Cross. This is what we decided to do. Our letter addressed to Joseph and Brenda Fenerman in New York City, in America, was the only knowledge of their location that we had. We gave this letter to the Red Cross on their next visit to our camp. The days at camp passed ever so slowly. Each night Rebecca and I would each go to our separate dormitories and then be reunited the next day at the breakfast food lines. We again were separated during the day because of our different work assignments. We then had our evening meal together, only to be separated again at bedtime. The war news was very sparse, but we did hear of the Nazi bombing of England and then the invasion of Russia by the Nazis.

So far all the war news was bad. You could see the depression on the faces of our fellow internees with each bad news report. Then near the end of 1941, we heard the news of Japan attacking the United States of America at a place called Pearl Harbor, and shortly after that of the declaration of war by Germany on the United States. Somehow we all took this news as positive, for it gave us hope of the final victory of the allies over the Nazis. The United States, at that time, was viewed as the ultimate sanctuary and hope for the down- trodden people of Europe.

The year of 1942 passed very slowly for us at camp. Our daily routines never seemed to change much. Then one day Rebecca and I were summoned to the camp directors office. We had a visitor. It was Adam Mendorer. Although we had only met him once at our grandson's birthday party at our daughters apartment, we both recognized him immediately. He had received permission to travel to our camp from the Swiss authorities. "I just had to talk to you in person", he told us. "I couldn't put any details of Sara's and Ari's death in writing as it would not go well with the Swiss if this information fell into the wrong hands." His explanation of the circumstances of our children's death then followed. "We had just about reached the Swiss border in our escape from Austria, when a German ski patrol spotted us and opened fire on our group. Sara was wounded by the German rifle fire. Ari then helped her until we reached the safety of Switzerland. By the time medical help arrived, it was too late to save her. She died with Ari there to comfort her last breath. Ari, Gretchen, and I were sent to an internment camp.

" Once there, Ari recruited three other young men, and the five of us vowed to take our revenge on the Nazis. We would sneak out of the camp and cross over to Austria. We then would steal weapons from the Nazis and attack the German ski patrols. With each successful raid we would accumulate more weapons and ammunition for our next border crossing raid. We would hide these weapons in a cave in the mountains for our next raid. We did this successfully for about a year, but finally on our last raid, Ari was killed providing a rear guard action for the rest of us. This put an end to these raids, as it was Ari who was our leader and inspiration. I just had to tell you all of these details about your children's deaths so that you would know that Ari was there to comfort Sara at her death and of the heroism of your son-in-law.

We thanked Adam, and he told us that he and Gretchen were interned together at camp, and would marry as soon as possible. We both hugged Adam and thanked him with tears in our eyes, and gave our blessings as he left. Somehow knowing the circumstances of our children's death did provide some measure of comfort to us.

The most important thing that was now our duty, was to someday reunite with our grandson, and guard the list of the Jewish children hidden at the convent orphanage. Both, Rebecca and I had memorized the seven other names and the Jewish surnames of the children on the list. When we would hear of someone in camp with that surname, we would very carefully and nonchalantly ask about their missing family members. None of these inquiries however indicated that any of them were linked to these Jewish children.

Finally, in 1943, the bits of war news started to get better. Success by the allies in Africa.

The tough resistance by the Russians on the eastern front. The news of the Americans and the British bombing of the Germans. It now appeared that the winds of war were more favorable to the allies. They were now on the offensive. Then the news of the successful allied invasion of the Italian island of Sicily was told to us by the Swiss workers at the camp directors office. This invasion which started on July 10, 1943, brought the allies almost back to the European continent. We took this news as a sign of the ultimate defeat of the Nazis. We now waited impatiently for the news that the allies invaded France. It would be another year before this happened.

CHAPTER VIII

The War Ends

The difficult daily routine at camp helped us take our minds off the lack of physical comforts, and helped us to pass the time of our confined internment. Rebecca and I were still billeted at different barrack dormitories as were most of the other couples without children and all of the singles. Rebecca just turned fifty seven years old. She is about a year and a half younger than I. There are no birthday parties at internment camps, just my kiss and best wishes for her. We still waited to receive word that our letter to Joseph and Brenda Fenerman had been successful in locating them in New York City, in America. We started to receive more frequent reports at camp of how the war was progressing. Then came the news of Italy's armistice with the allies in September of 1943, and the occupation of Italy by German troops.

The winter of 1943 arrived, and it was very cold. Someone at camp said that this was good for the Russian defenders of their homeland. Being a former History teacher, I knew this to be true. Napoleon found this out when he raided Russia in the past. Then one day a new internee arrived at camp. This recent escapee from Poland told us of the round up of all the Jews and the shipping them off in railroad boxcars to unknown destinations. This was very upsetting to us and to the other Jews at camp. We all wondered what their fate would be. It was then that I recalled the comment by the old gentleman at temple, after the warning by our Rabbi, when he said, "After all, they can't kill all of us." I was so glad that Rebecca and I had left Austria when we did, and so grateful to Rebecca's friend, Sister Margaret, for hiding us and our grandson.

I reached into my pocket to get my wallet so that I could retrieve the list given to me by Sister Margaret. Although I knew the contents of the list by heart, it somehow gave me comfort just to look at it.

New Years Day 1944 came, but there were no celebrations as in pre Nazi days. All we at camp could do is try to survive the harsh conditions and very cold weather. It seemed to me that at the coldest part of every winter at camp is when the greatest number of deaths occurred. This would probably be true whether at camp or at our homes, but being away from home only made this sad time for their loved ones worse.

Then just before the approach of spring, the Red Cross arrived at camp with their usual gifts of survival, but on this occasion there was also a letter for us from America. Our letter to Joseph and Brenda Fenerman had been received, and this was their response. We were glad that our letter to them was delivered, but sad at the terrible news that we had to give them. They thanked us for letting them know about Ari and Sara, and they wanted to know why nothing was in the letter about their grandson Jonathan. They also requested that if we could provide a more detailed account of their son and daughter-in-laws deaths. We didn't want to put anything in writing about Jonathan, as it might fall into the wrong hands and jeopardize his safety. They would have to wait for more definite information. We did however, hurriedly write a letter to them that information about Jonathan's whereabouts would come at a later date. We also gave them a more complete account of Sara and Ari's deaths that we were unaware of in our previous letter. We hoped that the circumstances of their deaths would give them some measure of comfort when they were told of Ari's heroism, as it did for us.

We gave this letter to the Red Cross workers before they left camp to mail to America, this time with a more complete address. Then just before the start of summer, the news came to camp like a flash of lightening. The allies had invaded France on June 6, 1944.

This news brought a smile to everyone's face in our camp, and we could only hope that the defeat of Germany and the Nazis was near. With this positive turn of events, the atmosphere at the camp seemed to be much happier. It had been a very long time since we had seen smiles on anyone,s face, and it felt good to observe this. With every visit to our camp by anyone, the internees would bombard them with numerous questions about the war news, and of the latest allied successes. The happy time at camp was followed by the terrible news of the Nazi counterattacks in France in December of 1944, called The Battle of the Bulge. We all prayed that there would be no victory for our enemy. Then the news came that the Germans had been repulsed and the allied victory was near. The winter months of 1944 passed quickly with the anticipation that this war would finally be over.

It was near the end of April when we heard that Russia had taken Austria, and that Vienna was in their hands. May 7, 1945 came and we were immediately told of Germany's surrender to the allies. We all wondered when we could go home. We were told that we must stay in the internment camp until the authorities in our country could restore some order out of the chaos of the recent events. Travel would be difficult on roads jammed with the military and displaced refugees. There was no infrastructure in place to care for the thousands seeking to return to their homes.

Austria was divided into four occupation zones. One zone for each of the allied countries fighting the Germans. These were the American, British, French, and Russian zones. Vienna was in the Russian zone. The decision to split up Austria's occupation at wars end was decided at a conference meeting held at the estate called the Livadia near Yalta, a famous Black Sea resort in the Crimea. The three countries represented at this conference were the United States, Great Britian, and Russia, called the big three. This would not make it easy to return to our home in Vienna. The anxiety of waiting for word that we would be aloud to return home was very stressful on everyone at camp, and seemed to make the time drag very slowly. Finally word came that we could start our journey back to our home in Vienna. New identity papers, travel permits, and backpacks with some necessities were provided by the Swiss government, The Red Cross, and American relief agencies, along with train travel coupons. We didn't have any idea of what lay ahead, except that we were returning to our home in Vienna, and to our grandson.

Just before leaving camp we posted a letter to Ari's parents in America, that we were on our way back to Vienna to retrieve our grandson Jonathan at the convent orphanage of The Sister's of Saint Paul. The Mother Superior of the convent was Sister Margaret, who was my wife's childhood friend. We owe our gratitude to her for hiding our grandson and others from the Nazis. We also explained that we couldn't give them this information sooner as we were afraid of this falling into the wrong hands, and endangering the Jewish children and their benefactors.

CHAPTER IX

Searching For Our Grandson

The morning of our departure from the internment camp was very hectic. Everyone was milling about in what seemed to me as if in a confusing manner. Finally as the internees started to leave camp the confusion subsided and the atmosphere was calmer. Rebecca and I made our rounds to the various camp workers and internees that we had bonded with in our long confinement to bid our farewells, and to thank them for their kindness during our stay at camp. The first leg of our journey back home was by foot to the railroad station at Landeck in Austria. This was a very long journey, and took about a week for the younger travelers and twice as long for us older folks. It was fortunate that this journey was taking place in the warm months of summer, but it still was very difficult for us at night. Sleeping along the side of the road with only our bedroll to keep us warm, and a canvas tarp to protect us from the rain. There was however, some comfort in the safety of traveling with so many of the other refugees. The journey through Switzerland was hard on us, but once we entered Austria the conditions were very bad. The number of refugees increased, and their gaunt appearance indicated the misery that they had endured. In addition to the refugees, there were countless military convoys on the roads and we had to move out of their way when they passed. When we finally arrived in Landeck, we were both exhausted and wondered if we would ever get back to our home in Vienna. Our stay in Landeck wasn't too bad as it gave us a chance to rest up a little. The American military also provided us with food and medical assistance to those refugees that required it. After about three days of waiting it was finally our turn to board the train to Innsbruck.

The train was packed so tightly with passengers, and the smell of people unable to properly bathe wasn't very nice, but still much better than walking along crowded roads. We passed through Innsbruck, and then proceeded east across the country, passing through each city and town until we finally were home in Vienna. As soon as we left the train we were greeted by the Russian military occupiers of our city. They herded us into long lines, and carefully checked everyones identity papers and travel permits. When our turn came to be checked, we were thoroughly questioned and given a permit to return home, if it was still there. We were told that there may be others residing there who also had permits from the Russians, because of the housing shortage caused by the recent bombings and military battles. With our papers all stamped and approved by the Russians, we started the long walk to our house, past all the debris of the war. Our small house was still there. To us this seemed like a miracle. When we opened the front door we were confronted by two other couples who were living there with Russian permits. After showing our permit they were forced to accept our right to live there. We told them that this was our home before the war, but that didn't seem to phase them at all. The place was a mess and the two couples living there were very unkempt. My thoughts went back to the day we left our home, and Rebecca had made such an effort to make sure that all was in order and neat and clean. I looked at my wife and could see the frustration on her face. We took possession of one small room that formally was our daughter Sara's bedroom, and gave a blind eye to the rest of the house and also to the other two couples. At least we would have a roof over our heads.

Our first thoughts were to go to the convent to see Sister Margaret and retrieve our grandson, but everyone was required to report in the mornings to the Russians for work assignments for cleanup of war debris and to be given our daily rations of food. When the weekend came we had our first opportunity to go to the convent. When we arrived at the convent, we were told that Sister Margaret had died two years ago. There was no orphanage or home for the aged at the convent. They had ceased to exist with the death of Sister Margaret. None of the nuns we questioned could tell us what had become of the orphan children or their whereabouts. We could not get any clue that might help us find where they had been taken. Many of the nuns that we talked to, did recall that we worked at the old age home in the convent, but we both sensed a secretive attitude from the nuns.

With deep despair we returned to our house with no idea of where to go from here. The following day we returned to our conscripted duties for various cleanup of war damage, and provided rations to keep us alive. At least Rebecca and I were together, and each of us relied on the other for moral support and hope that we would locate our grandson. Rebecca suggested that we write Ari's father Joseph, in America. We should give him all the details of Jonathan's stay in the convent orphanage. Perhaps he could help, and he should also know that his grandson is missing and may still be alive. Getting this letter to America would be very difficult. The Russian were not going to let any correspondence through their jurisdiction. We didn't know why, but it was evident that the cooperation between them and the rest of the allies was nonexistent.

I took the list out of my wallet and stared at the names of the eight Jewish children. I wondered what our next move would be to locate our grandson. Rebecca perceiving my despair, said that if we could locate Sister Lucille, maybe she could help us. Recalling how pleasant she was, I told her that this sounded like a good idea. We returned to the convent as soon as we were able, and inquired about her whereabouts. After extensive prodding, one of the nuns let it slip out that she was stationed at an outpatient medical clinic that was located at the parish of Saint Mary's in Vienna. What luck, we thought. Rebecca said, perhaps Sister Lucille could get some mail through the Russian zone to America. We very carefully wrote our letter to Joseph Fenerman with the details of the Jewish children that were on the list given to me by Sister Margaret with the anticipation of locating Sister Lucille. This is the first time that I dared to share the list with anyone, but now we were desperate.

At the first opportunity, we sought out the outpatient clinic at St. Mary's. There she was, looking a little bit older, but still with her pleasant personality. On seeing us, a huge smile appeared on her face. She said that she thought of us often, and wondered how we had made out in Switzerland during the war years. She then said that the memory of our escape from the Nazis, always made her feel good. After telling her of our experience in the past years, we asked her about Sister Margaret, and what she knew of the orphanage children. The orphanage was the first to go. The children were sent to another Catholic orphanage in Salzburg, at the parish of Saint Stephen's. Sister Margaret protested but was unable to change the minds of the diocese. Sister Lucille said that she didn't know if Sister Margaret had informed the diocese of the Jewish children being hidden there. She then told us that as the population of the old age home in the convent decreased, it was decided to move the remaining few to different locations. Shortly after these occurrences, Sister Margaret had a heart attack and passed away. Sister Lucille said that after the orphanage and home for the aged had been removed from the convent, she seemed to be very depressed and she always seemed sad.

We then asked Sister Lucille if there was a possibility of her getting a letter out of the country, past the Russian zone, to be mailed to America. She said that perhaps one of the priests would take it with him when he next travels to Rome and mail it for us from there. We quickly added the information about Jonathan's last known location to the letter to Joseph, sealed it and gave it to Sister Lucille. She promised us that she would see to it that it was delivered. We both thanked her for her past and present kindness, and we all exchanged hugs. She invited us to visit her again, when possible in these hard times.

When we returned home, the two couples sharing our house were arguing, and accusing each other of stealing their belongings. This chaotic atmosphere was a constant tribulation at our house, and the whole country seemed to be in a state of chaos. This was not a pleasant time to be living in Vienna. We were powerless to do anything about it, except to grin and bear the frustration of the times. Every weekday morning we both would go to the designated work place that the Russian occupation officials sent us to put in our days work, and receive our rations and script money for our survival. Weekends were free to us to try to improve our living standards. The time passed slowly as we waited for some news from America. The arguments between the two couples living in our house seemed to be more violent. It was obvious that the escalation of these frequent arguments would end in disaster for both couples.

There was nothing we could do to stop this crazy behavior. Our attempts to mediate these arguments only seemed to make matters worse. We decided that the best thing we could do was to avoid them as much as we could.

On one weekend visit to Sister Lucille, she told us that our letter was on its way to America. I tried to get permission from the Russians for Rebecca and I to travel to Salzburg to see if we could locate our grandson, but they refused. Things seemed hopeless.

Then, in November of 1945, elections for a newly formed government were held by the Austrians with permission of the allied occupation forces. This was a good sign, but we still had the Russian occupation forces in our zone making all the decisions. Winter was very bleak for Rebecca and I, but we could see the gradual improvement of conditions in the country. Spring of 1946 came, and with it a visit from a Russian intelligence officer. We were questioned about our relationship to an American named Joseph Fenerman. After a thorough interrogation we were given travel permits to visit him in Salzburg. Salzburg was in the American occupation zone of occupied Austria. We immediately made preparations for this trip. It would take what little money we had to pay for the rail tickets to meet Joseph in Salzburg as directed in the letter from him as given to us by the Russian intelligence officer. When we left our house we wondered if this would be the last time we would see it. Not having to live with the two couples sharing our house, would be a welcomed blessing.

Before going to the railroad station, we had two stops that we both felt that we must make. The first stop was at the site of our temple. The Nazis had destroyed it, but we felt that we must take this last opportunity to reminisce at the site that we had worshiped at for so many years. Our next stop was at St. Mary's clinic to say goodbye to Sister Lucille and to thank her for all of her kindness. On our way to the rail station we took in the sites of Vienna, both knowing that this would be the last time that we would be at the city that we both grew up in. At the rail station we had no trouble from the authorities, and boarded the train to Salzburg. When we finally arrived in Salzburg, we went to the station masters office as we had been previously directed to do, and he gave us directions to the hotel where Joseph was staying. Our funds were gone, so we walked to the hotel. The walk from the station to the hotel was very long and it was fortunate that our backpacks were the only thing we had to carry. At the hotel we went to the check in counter and asked for Joseph Fenerman. The clerk telephoned him and he immediately came to greet us. He was dressed in a very expensive looking suit, and looked like he had not aged a day older than last we saw him ten years earlier in December of 1936. We both commented on how well he looked. Rebecca remarked that America must agree with you. Joseph told us how happy he was to see us, and glad that we were able to survive the terrible war. We asked how his wife Brenda and his parents, Simon and Golda were. He told us that they were all fine and in good health. It was obvious to Rebecca and I that Joseph was saddened by our appearance in our ragged apparel. He hugged us both and I noticed a tear in his eye.

Joseph asked if we had eaten lunch. I told him that on our way here we had passed a church that was giving lunch to refugees. Rebecca and I stopped there and had something to eat. He then told us that he had reserved a room for us at the hotel, and that he was sure that we would like to freshen up and get some rest after our long trip. He then told us that he would have some new clothes sent to our room. We thanked him for his kindness, and I perceived that he was aware of our lack of funds. On the way to our room he told us that he had gone to the orphanage at St. Stephens parish. He spoke to a Sister Phyllis. He showed her our letter about the Jewish children that had been hidden from the Nazis at the convent orphanage of the Sister's of Saint Paul. Joseph then told us that they denied any knowledge of any Jewish children, and was treated very abruptly. He suggested that we all make another attempt to convince this nun to consider our claim about these Jewish children. He told us that he had little hope of changing this nuns mind after the way he was treated, so he sent a telegram to a Jewish Refugee Agency in New York City, in America, to solicit their help.

When we reached our room, Joseph paused at the door and became very emotional as he proceeded to tell us the news reports and evidence of the Holocaust of our Jewish brethren. The rumors that we heard in no way anticipated how terrible things actually were. We entered our room and Joseph said that he would return for us at dinner time. The room was very luxurious and must have cost Joseph a great deal of money in these hard times. The first thing we did was to take advantage of the beautiful bathing facilities.

After our baths, we both dressed and lounged about the very beautiful hotel room that Joseph had provided for us. Rebecca remarked that he must be very wealthy and influential to be able to procure such a luxurious room in these hard times. There was a knock on the door and a hotel employee delivered a large package of new clothes with a note from Joseph saying that he hoped everything would fit us. How he was able to obtain these clothes on such short notice was very puzzling to us. We hadn't felt this pampered in years. This was the first time since we left our home in Vienna in 1938, that we felt indulgent.

Just before the dinner hour arrived, Joseph came to our room. He remarked how nice we both looked in our new clothes, and asked if everything fit properly. We both expressed our gratitude for his many kindnesses. We then all went to the hotel dining room and were treated to a wonderful meal. After a long conversation of each of us telling our experience during the war years, we made plans to go to the orphanage on the following morning. With our additional evidence and testimony, perhaps this Sister Phyllis would be more receptive to us. We parted company, and went to our room with the promise to be ready early the next morning.

CHAPTER X

Help From Abroad

When Joseph came to our room the next morning, we were both ready, and we all went down to the hotel dining room for a quick breakfast. We then all went directly to the orphanage at Saint Stephen's convent. After being admitted to the waiting room by a young nun, Sister Phyllis arrived. I immediately noticed the abrupt attitude that Joseph had told us that she exhibited on his previous encounter. I told her of our stay at the convent of the Sisters of Saint Paul in Vienna, and showed her the list of Jewish children given to us by Sister Margaret. She responded very sternly, and told us that she had identity documents on all the children in her orphanage, and there were no Jewish children there. She told us not to return to her orphanage, and we were very rudely shown to the door. We left the convent and went next door to the church rectory building and knocked on the front door. This time we were admitted with a cordial manner by the housekeeper, and told to wait in the front hall while she summoned the parish priest. Soon a short stocky priest appeared, and greeted us with a pleasant smile. He told us that his name was Father Herman. We introduced ourselves and told him the reason for our visit. He told us that Sister Phyllis had told him of Joseph's previous visit, and was aware of our search for our grandson. He suggested that we take our case directly to the Bishop of the diocese and the governing board for the orphanage. He then was kind enough to give us directions to the Bishop's residence. We left Father Herman and went directly to make our case to the Bishop.

The Bishop's residence was across town from the orphanage, and it was fortunate that we had a cab for our trip. We were admitted to the Bishop's residence by a security guard. He told us to have a seat in the very large and opulent foyer while he called the Bishop's secretary on his intercom, and told him the reason for our visit. While we sat there waiting, we could see other rooms beyond the foyer, and were impressed by their beauty. It was apparent that the war hadn't touched this building. After a long wait, the Bishop's secretary came to the foyer and introduced himself. He told us to follow him, and he escorted us to the Bishop's office. The secretary then made introductions to our party, the Bishop, and his legal counsel, who was also present. The Bishop's name was Henry Fernburg, and he started the conversation by telling us that Sister Phyllis and Father Herman had informed his office of our search for our grandson. While he said that he was sympathetic to our cause, we had no legal proof to claim that our grandson was in their orphanage. I repeated the whole story of Rebecca's relationship with Sister Margaret, and her offer to hide us and our grandson from the Nazis. Then I showed the Bishop the list that Sister Margaret gave me with the names of the eight Jewish children, with their fake names and birth dates. I told him that if he would check the names of the children that came from Sister Margaret's orphanage, he would be able to authenticate the list that she gave me. His response was that all that he could go by was the legal identity documents that he had for all the children. I told him that Sister Margaret had to forge these documents to hide the children from the Nazis. He just shook his head and said that I would need to have more proof than my word and a time worn piece of paper before he would consider our claim.

Ari's father listened intently while I was pleading my case to the Bishop. When the Bishop rebuffed my testimony, he came to our defense. In a very eloquent manner he told the Bishop that it was apparent that he had predetermined that he would deny our claim for the return of our grandson and the other Jewish children, no matter how convincing our evidence. He then said, "I can tell by the look on your face that you know our list of the Jewish children is authentic, and this audience that you give to hear our claim is nothing but a charade." Joseph then told the Bishop, that he could be sure that a higher authority would be called upon to decide this case. The Bishop responded by telling us that this meeting was over, and asked us to please leave at once. The Bishop's secretary then hurriedly escorted us out of the building. I remarked to Joseph that it was apparent that the Bishop hadn't endured any hardship during the war. We started to walk back to the hotel, but were lucky enough to flag down a cab to bring us to the hotel. When we arrived at the hotel, it was the dinner hour, and we all went to the dining room. During our meal, Joseph told us that tomorrow we would all go to the American legation office and obtain travel visas for us to leave Austria and first go to Rome, Italy and then on to America, when our business in Rome was complete. He told us that he had contacts at the American Embassy that would make this possible.

My recollection of Joseph when we first met years ago was a person of average intelligence with a laid back personality. It was obvious that his ten years in America had made him a very confident person. It was apparent that he was quite successful, and America was good to him.

The next morning we met in the hotel dining room for a quick breakfast, and then we all went to the American legation office. Joseph handled everything and guided us through the various interviews and we soon had the travel permits and visas that we required. It became very obvious that Joseph had extensive influence and connections. After this business was taken care of, Rebecca and I returned to the hotel and Joseph went to the cable office to send some telegrams to America. He later told us that he had contacted the Jewish Refugee Agency in New York City, to solicit their help in dealing with the Catholic authorities at the Vatican in Rome. This Jewish agency was very busy trying to help the hundreds of Jewish refugees with no place to go, to find a home in Isreal, but they agreed to provide representation for us in our claim to the Vatican. They told Joseph that there were many reports coming from all over Europe of similar situations of Jewish children placed in Christian orphanages to hide them from the Nazis, and the difficulty parents were having in getting their children returned. In many of these cases there were no surviving relatives to claim these children. This was a much larger issue than just our case. They were eager to start negotiations with the Vatican on these reports. Our claim would be the first case in this matter.

When Joseph returned to the hotel he called our room, and we all met in the hotel dining room for dinner. This had been a very productive day and our expectations for success in getting our grandson returned, were encouraged. Joseph told us that we would leave Salzburg in the morning after breakfast, and travel by train to Rome.

The train station was also crowded, and once again, Joseph exhibited his influential connections by getting us past the crowds to the train.

The train was very crowded. The priority passes that Joseph had obtained for our trip guaranteed our seats for the entire trip. The rail stations at every stop were jammed with refugees heading south. Their condition was tragic. Their faces drawn with frustration, their clothing ragged, their stature bent with despair. It was not much different when we crossed over into Italy. The food shortages and lack of goods and necessities was all over Europe. The only supplies of food and materials were coming from America and England. The war and the Nazis had stripped these countries bare. It would take a huge effort to get these European countries back on their feet.

Traveling with Joseph, with his political connections, was a huge advantage. I couldn't resist asking Joseph the source of his influence. He said that his brother Joshua was very wealthy. He was the chief executive officer of a large accounting firm, and was on the board of directors for many other large firms. He told us that Joshua took him into his firm at an executive level, and he together with his brother, had many influential friends and access to many important and powerful people. This satisfied my curiosity. When I compared myself to the plight of the refugees, I felt ashamed at my good fortune. Many of these refugees were Jews who somehow had eluded the mass killing of their brethren by the Nazis. They were traveling to Palestine, which was their final destination. Their hope was to regain their homeland. The British occupiers of Palestine had forbidden this migration, but by various means, this migration to their homeland continued. Summer of 1946 was just beginning when we arrived in Rome. With the generosity of Joseph, we were set up in a hotel which was no small fete in these hard times.

This was another example of Joseph's powerful friends, and what seemed to me, his unlimited resources. After Rebecca and I were settled in, Joseph had set up a meeting with two officials who were from the Jewish Refugee Agency, based in America, in New York City. They were to be our political ally with our dealings with the Catholic

Church at the Vatican. This refugee agency was only one of many Jewish agencies in America that were involved in discussions with the Vatican on various topics pertaining to the Nazi and Fascist crimes against the Jews during the war. Many Jews felt that the Catholic Church and the Vatican didn't put enough pressure on the Nazis and the Fascists to stop their genocide of the Jews during the war. There also were many reports from all over Europe that many church dioceses were not being cooperative with Jewish families seeking the return of their children placed in orphanages to hide them from the Nazis and Fascists. The Pope's representatives at the Vatican denied the allegations that they could have stopped the genocide of the Jews, and were quick to promise to fully cooperate in the return of Jewish children placed in their care. The Vatican took a defensive position on this issue, so as not to antagonize the Jewish people any further. They granted us an audience with an aid to the Pope's secretary. We all met in his office in the Vatican at the appointed time. Our group consisted of two pro bono lawyers from the refugee agency, Joseph, Rebecca, and myself. After the Pope's secretary took testimony from the lawyers and Joseph, it was my turn to speak. I took out my wallet where I carefully kept the original list given to me by Sister Margaret seven years ago. I carefully handed the list to the secretary. I asked the Vatican Counsel Secretary to look at the eight names of the Jewish children on the list with their date of birth, and their fake Christian names given to them by Sister Margaret. I asked him how else could I have come by this list and information if not given to me by Sister Margaret. How could anyone doubt the authenticity of the list and undo the very brave and good deeds of this holy nun. The secretary looked intently at the list and I perceived the look of belief in his eyes. He asked if there was anyone who could corroborate the authenticity of the list given to me by the deceased nun. I told him that Sister Lucille, who was stationed at Saint Mary's medical clinic in Vienna, would testify to the truth of our testimony and the validity of the list. I told the secretary that it would be very difficult to get her testimony because Vienna is in the Russian occupation zone of Austria. He responded that he could arrange to get her testimony by having one of the Vatican's clergy visit her in Vienna without informing the diocese in both Vienna and Salzburg.

I told the secretary that our grandson Jonathan would now be almost ten years old. The other Jewish children on the list would be eight to ten years old. I pleaded with him to restore our children to us. He promised that he and the Pope, who was aware of our case and the poor treatment we had experienced by the diocese in Salzburg, was sympathetic to us, and the Vatican would act promptly on this matter. The secretary then copied the information on the list, which I wouldn't part with. At this point in the meeting the two lawyers from the Jewish Refugee Agency, proceeded to give their testimony of this case and the numerous other cases that they were investigating on the behalf of other clients.

They told the Vatican secretary of the difficulty they had experienced in dealing with the Catholic Church in these matters. They told him that there were numerous other reports coming from all over Europe about Jewish children who had been hidden from the Nazis in seminaries, orphanages, and infant care sections of Christian hospitals. We are being stone-walled by officials in these places in our efforts to restore our children to their Jewish heritage. There are no lists in most of these cases, but evidence will be obtained, you can be sure. We urge the Vatican to urge these various places of refuge to be more cooperative with the many Jewish agencies seeking the return of their children. The secretary responded by again repeating the Pope's awareness of these reports and his sympathy and assurance that the Vatican would act promptly in resolving these matters.

We all left the Vatican and Rebecca and I, together with Joseph, returned to our hotel to wait in suspense for some word from the Vatican or Jewish Refugee Agency. During this time Joseph had made contact with the American Embassy to obtain entry visas for Rebecca and I to enter America. We were very grateful and not sad to leave Austria. It was about three weeks later that we heard that Sister Lucille's testimony was taken by the Vatican and supported our claim. We were told that the Pope himself had directed that the Catholic diocese in Salzburg return all eight children on the list, and be given custody to the Jewish Refugee Agency. Joseph would be given legal custody of Jonathan, and the other seven children would be placed in the custody of the Jewish Refugee Agency to search for any survivors of their families and or to arrange for them to be adopted by Jewish families in America. Joseph left Rebecca and I in Rome while he and officials from the agency went to Salzburg to retrieve our children.

CHAPTER XI

Reunion

Our wait in Rome for some word from Joseph on the return of our grandson was very stressful. Before going to Salzburg, Joseph had warned Rebecca and I of the dangers of straying far from our hotel. He pointed out that the poverty of both the Italians and the refugees passing through Rome on their way to various places in search of some sort of security and a better way of life, would observe what they perceived to be our affluence, and possibly could be a danger to us. The time passed very slowly. There was just so much we could do around the hotel. Gradually we found that we were straying further away from the hotel. The Nazis in their occupation of Italy, had stripped the country bare of food, goods, and seriously damaged the infrastructure. The Americans and the British occupation forces were bringing supplies of food, medicine, and goods, as fast as they could, but such a large undertaking as this would take quite a bit of time before they could get the country back on its feet. The plight of the Italians and the refugees was heartbreaking for us to observe. Many of the refugees were Jews who somehow had escaped the Nazi genocide in the death camps. On our daily walks from the hotel we would occasionally talk with the refugees and Italians. We came to find out that many of the Jewish refugees were seeking to go to Palestine The British were in charge of governing and military occupation of this territory. They had prohibited any migration of Jews into this land. The Arab residents of

Palestine outnumbered the Jewish residents, and they wanted to keep it that way. The pressure on the British to stop the migration of the Jewish refugees by the Arabs was intense. This didn't stop them as we came to find out by our many conversations with them. Somehow they secured the help to finance the procurement of freighters and boats of every description for their illegal trip in the Mediterranean Sea to create a new homeland in the land of their ancestors. These refugees had nothing, only their lives, but they were willing to risk even that to finally return to their homeland. It wouldn't be until November 29, 1947, when the United Nations voted to end the control of Palestine by the British and divide the country into a Jewish state and an Arab state, that this would happen. The Jews agreed to the United Nations plan, but the Arabs didn't. They wanted all of Palestine. All the nearby Arab nations prepared to go to war against the Jews. On May 14, 1948, the British control of Palestine ended and the state of Isreal was born. The next day Isreal was attacked by five arab nations.

It was during these daily walks from the hotel that Rebecca and I started to learn to speak Italian. Our daily exposure to the language made this easy. We both then decided to prepare for our immigration to America by learning to speak English. This gave us something to do while we waited for Joseph.

It was near the end of summer of 1946 when Joseph returned to Rome. That morning when he knocked on our hotel room door, he had the most beautiful happy grin on his face. He told us that he had something wonderful to show us. We both accompanied him to a large suite on an upper floor of the hotel. On reaching the door of this suite, Joseph knocked on the door and a Jewish American nanny employed by the Jewish Refugee Agency came to the door and admitted us. There in the sitting room of the suite were eight children engaged in various playful activities, being supervised by another nanny.

We looked them over and Rebecca and I quickly recognized Jonathan. This was very easy because he was the image of his father.

These children would now be between eight and ten years old. They had been in these Catholic orphanages for eight years. The nanny that answered our knock on the door commented on how well behaved the children were. She said that the nuns who raised them in the orphanage must have done an excellent job in caring for them. This same nanny then told us that she had observed that the children all bonded very strongly with each other. She said that this was probably due to the lack of a parental figure to bond with.

Joseph called out to John and he turned his head in our direction. "Come here" he said to the boy, "I want to introduce you to your relatives." The child turned his head to the other nanny that was caring for them as if to see if this was permitted, and with a nod from her, he came over to us. It was obvious to Rebecca and I that he had been raised in a very strict enviroment with rigid disciplinary rules. When the boy stood there by us, Joseph said; " John Wickischer, do you recognize any of us?" The boy shook his head no. Joseph said to the boy that he had already told him that he was his father's father, and now I want you to meet your mother's father and mother. "We are your grandparents. Your real name is Jonathan Fenerman. Do you remember your mother and father?" The boy said no. Rebecca could resist no longer and gave Jonathan a hug. The boy somehow could sense the parental bonds with us, and without being directed, gave Joseph and I a hug. Rebecca had tears in her eyes. Joseph then told Jonathan that he and the other children were all coming to America with us.

We then walked over to the other children with Jonathan, and had him introduce us to all the other children. As he called out their names, I pictured their real Jewish names in my mind, from the list given to me by Sister Margaret so long ago. As we talked with Jonathan and the other children it became obvious to us that their communication with each other was very cheerful and loving. Their close association with each other, first at the orphanage in Vienna and then in Salzburg, had made the bond between them very strong. After the children are brought to America, and the search for any of their relatives who survived the war is completed, it would be best if the children could be kept together.

If no living relatives are found the transition to their adoption should be very gradual so as not to upset them. We visited with the children and talked to them about their interests for the entire morning. The nanny finally interrupted us, and told us it was time for their lunch. She told us that it would be best for the children to have an undisturbed meal, and that we could visit later. We left the children's hotel suite, but not before getting another hug from Jonathan and all of the other seven children.

Joseph, Rebecca, and I went down to the hotel dining room to have our lunch and to hear about Joseph's trip to Salzburg with the agency lawyers and the Pope's Vatican representatives. Rebecca and I listened intently as Joseph gave us the account of his trip.

Joseph said, " The Pope's representative had made the journey to Vienna without us because of the difficulty we would encounter from the Russians in getting entry and exit from their occupation zone. The Pope's instructions to his representatives must have been very explicit, because this man was definitely on our side in our efforts to get custody of our grandson and the other seven Jewish children on the list. When he met with the agency lawyers and me in Salzburg on his return from Vienna, he gave us the account of his trip. He told us that the Russians gave him no trouble in access and exit from their occupation zone with his cover story of being there only on church business. He first went to the convent of The Sister's of Saint Paul where he gathered testimony from them on their recollection of the convent orphanage and old age home that were formerly located there. He told us that everything that he had learned from them substantiated our account of past events. He then went to the medical clinic at Saint Mary's parish, and had an interview with Sister Lucille. She corroborated your entire story, and was happy to hear that you both were safe in Rome, and she told him to send her best wishes. He then told us that now we can confront the Bishop here in Salzburg, and The Pastor of Saint Stephen's Parish, and Sister Phyllis who was in charge of the convent orphanage."

"The Pope's representative, the two refugee agency lawyers, and I requested and were granted an appointment with the Bishop of the Salzburg diocese on the following day. When our group arrived at the Bishop's residence, we were very politely escorted to the office of Bishop Henry Fernburg. He was there with his secretary, and both of them had very sour looks on their faces in anticipation of being reprimanded by the Vatican. The Pope's representative, Father Dominic started the discussion. First he questioned the Bishop's reasons for not giving us a fair hearing on our request to be reunited with our grandson. Then he scolded him for ignoring our evidence."

"Both the Bishop and his secretary were bristling with anger, but did not dare to talk back to the Pope's representative. Their faces were a much bluer shade then when we first entered his office."

"Father Dominic then instructed the Bishop to prepare the necessary documents for the release of all eight Jewish children to the custody of the Jewish Refugee Agency lawyers.

He then told him that he would go to Saint Stephen's Parish on the following day and meet with Father Herman and Sister Phyllis to retrieve the children. Father Dominic turned face to face with the Bishop and repeated these words, "These are the Pope's orders, and expects that they be carried out without delay." With that business concluded, we all returned to our hotel to await the next day."

"On the following day we were met at the hotel by two Jewish American nanny's who both spoke German. The agency had sent them in anticipation of our success in getting custody of the children. We all went to Saint Stephen's Parish Orphanage, and were greeted by Father Herman and Sister Phyllis. They both had been given orders from the Bishop, and had sheepish looks on their faces. They were quick to expedite the release of the children to our custody. We then all went back to the hotel and made arrangements to leave Salzburg and return to Rome."

Rebecca then told Joseph at the conclusions of his report of the trip to Salzburg that she would have liked to have been there to see the look on Bishop Henry Fernburg's face when he was commanded to release the children to our custody. Joseph then told us that The Jewish Refugee Agency is making all the necessary arrangements for the transportation of our grandson and the other seven children to America. They will also try to locate any relatives of the other children.

Joseph then told us that he had to return to America as soon as possible, and Rebecca and I could go with him or wait and go with the agency nanny's and the children on the ships passage that had been secured for them. We told him that we would like to travel to America with the children if that was alright. Joseph said that he wished that he could go with us and the children, but pressing business made it necessary for him to return quickly.

It was only ten days later when the ships passage to America was obtained for us and the children. Rebecca and I had spent those ten days visiting with Jonathan and the other seven children as much as the nanny's would allow. Those ten days spent visiting with the children and the ship voyage across the Atlantic Ocean to America were wonderful. We became acquainted with all the children and observed the very strong bonds that they had to each other. Their long years together in the convent orphanage had made them rely on each other for their emotional needs. When we arrived in the New York City harbor and passed the Statue Of Liberty, Rebecca and I both felt a sense of happiness and belonging. We were met at the dock by the agency lawyers and Joseph with his wife Brenda. They guided all of us through customs and made our entry to our new country as easy as possible.

The refugee agency tried to locate survivors of the children's parents and relatives, but Jonathan was the only one who had living relatives. The seven other children were all quickly adopted by Jewish families. Jonathan was adopted legally by Joseph and Brenda. Joseph had been very successful with business ventures with his brother Joshua and had the means to provide for Jonathan and insure that he would have the opportunity to go to college. Joseph and his wife Brenda were naturalized citizens and guided Rebecca and I through the process of becoming American citizens. Both my wife and I were quickly learning to speak English. This made our assimilation into the American way of life much easier. Joseph got us started in this new land by renting us a small apartment on Long Island, New York. Our apartment was located in a community where many other Jewish families lived. There was a temple and a Jewish Community Center nearby. With Joseph's influence, both Rebecca and I were given jobs at the Jewish center. Rebecca worked in the center library, and I conducted continuing education classes in History. These jobs gave both of us the opportunity to make good use of our previous job experience. These jobs provided enough money to support us comfortably without burdening others. Joseph's home was in another area of Long Island where the more affluent lived, as was evidence of his prosperity in America. Joseph's brother Joshua also lived in this affluent area. Joseph's daughter Rachael, Ari's younger sister, was just finishing medical school, and soon would be a licensed doctor. We were frequently invited to Joseph and Brenda's home on holiday and birthday occasions, and we were able to see the development of Jonathan into a young man. The seven other Jewish orphans that were rescued by the refugee agency were all adopted by affluent Jewish families living near Joseph and Joshua. Joshua and his wife had adopted one of the little girls brought to America with Jonathan. On some occasions when invited to Joseph's special events we were in the company of his neighbors who had adopted the other children, and were so pleased to see the development of the children. Their close bond to each other seemed to grow closer through the years.

CHAPTER XII

New Beginnings

It was spring of 1958, Rebecca and I had been in America for almost twelve years. We were both U.S. citizens, and were happy to be here in America to enjoy our senior years. We are both in our seventies and in good health. Rebecca and I are still working at the Jewish Community Center because the work load was light and made us feel like we were helping others. We also felt that it was good for us to keep working, and helping to keep us young and allowing us to keep in touch with others. The days came and went with pleasant repetition. We felt very fortunate to have each other and good friends, and to be able to watch Jonathan grow into manhood. Joseph and his wife Brenda had been wonderful for our grandson, and very kind and generous to us. Life had become beautiful in spite of the sadness of losing our daughter Sara and son-in-law Ari to the Nazis.

As I reflected back on my life here in America, there are many things that stand out in my memory that make me thank God for his blessings. I vividly recall the day when Joseph and Brenda took Rebecca and I to a New York Yankees baseball game. It was a beautiful and warm sunny afternoon, and even though Rebecca and I didn't understand the rules of baseball, the excitement of the huge packed stadium, and the food and beer, made a lasting impression on us. Then at the seventh inning there was a pause in the game which Joseph called the seventh inning stretch. A voice came over the loudspeaker asking for a moment of silent prayer for the American troops overseas, and to announce that Kate Smith would now sing God Bless America. Then without any direction, everyone stood up with hand placed over their heart, and observed the moment of prayer. Then, as Kate Smith's voice sang God Bless America, a multi-tude of American flags appeared. I remarked to our group what a wonderful show of patriotism this was.

On another occasion I recall the day at the community center when Rebecca came over to my work area to introduce me to an elderly couple who were at the same internment camp in Switzerland as we were. As hard as I tried I could not remember them. After we conversed for awhile and he told me of his work assignments at the camp, I then started to remember him and his wife. The younger couple that I now remembered at the camp had aged quite a lot, and it was evident that the years had not been easy for them. If Rebecca and I didn't have a benefactor like Joseph to help make life easier for us, we too would probably look much older also. That evening at home when we talked about the chance meeting that day with the couple from the internment camp, we both reminisced about our days at the camp. I pray to God that those days never happen again.

It was still early spring of 1958 when a visiting official from Israel was making a tour of Jewish American communities and centers. His name was Adam Mendorer. The cease fire agreements between Israel and their Arab neighbors was not going to well. The recent war in 1956 between

Israel and Egypt had made very little headway in restoring peace to the region. The United Nations peacemakers were the only thread that was keeping the war from starting again. The official was here in America to alert Jewish Americans to the dangers that Israel was facing, and to ask for funds for their defense. It was depressing to hear of the acts of terrorism that were being committed against the Jews.

It was very nice to once again meet with Adam. Rebecca and I felt very close to him, even though we had only met with him twice. Once at our grandson Jonathan's first birthday party, which he attended with his girlfriend, Gretchen Goldberg. The second time that we met was at the internment camp in Switzerland, when he visited us to explain to us the circumstances of Ari's and Sara's deaths. I asked Adam what happened to his girlfriend Gretchen, and how he had become an official of the Israeli defense department. He told us that he and Gretchen had decided to join the thousands of other Jewish refugees making their way to Palestine because they both felt that there wasn't any future for them in Austria. They were married in Israel and both joined the army as did all others who were able. They were both sent to the same kabotze and both helped in it's defense when they were attacked by the Arabs. He told us that they had one son, who they named Ari in honor of our son. This brought tears to Rebecca's eyes, and she gave Adam a huge hug. We then talked for some time about his experience in Israel, and how he rose in rank in the army. We then talked and reminisced about our time in Austria before the Nazi takeover, and our time spent in the internment camp in Switzerland. We invited him to have dinner at our home, but his travel itinerary would not allow him time to do so. He invited us to visit Gretchen and him at their home in Israel. I responded that we would love to visit, and who knows, perhaps some day this will come to pass, if God permits.

One weekend morning after our breakfast and reading the morning papers, I went down-stairs to our mailbox to get the mail. I brought it back to our apartment, and as I looked through the usual junk mail, I saw two letters addressed to us. One of the letters was an invitation from Joseph and Brenda to attend a college graduation party for Jonathan. A hand written note on the invitation card said that a limousine would be sent to pick us up at the time noted, as he knew that we had no transportation. Living in the neighborhood close to our jobs at the Jewish Community Center, and within walking distance to shopping and temple made it unnecessary to own a car. "How nice", remarked Rebecca, "They are always so thoughtful." The other letter was from Austria. It was from Sister Lucille in Vienna. In her letter she said that she was finally able to get our address with the help of a visiting priest to the hospital where she worked. This visiting priest was from the Vatican in Rome, and was acquainted with Father Dominic who had taken testimony from her regarding us many years ago. She told us that she was now in charge of the nursing staff at this Catholic hospital. She often thought back to our time together during the war years, and our flight from Austria to Switzerland. She wondered how we were, and if we were successful in getting our grandson returned to us. Rebecca and I were thrilled to hear from her, and my wife immediately took pen in hand to respond to her. She filled her in on the events of our getting our grandson and the other Jewish children from the orphanage returned, and our trip to America. She told her of our life here in America, and how the children had all made out. Finally she told her how happy we were to hear from her, and to please write again soon.

On the day of the graduation party, at the appointed time, our doorbell rang. The chauffeur who had been hired by Joseph to drive us to the graduation party was there to pick us up. Rebecca and I were ready, both dressed in our best attire, as we followed him to the limousine. The weather on that June day of 1958 was exceptionally beautiful. This was very fortunate as Joseph and Brenda had a huge outdoor party planned on their estate. Their home on Long Island was in an area where there were huge homes on large lots and occupied by very affluent people. There was a huge party tent set up for the guests. There were elaborate decorations everywhere, including balloons, flowers, lanterns, and garlands. Their home was also open to the guests for their refreshment as needed. Everything looked beautiful. Tables under the tent were set up with name tags and floral center-pieces. The place settings at the tables were very fancy. The caterers had serving areas set up, and there were beverage bars with protective canopies. There was overhead garden lanterns strung over the entire area, and there was a bandstand and dance floor over to one side. The overall setting looked like those fancy rich parties that I have seen in the movies. There were eight guests to a circular table. We were seated with Simon and Golda Fenerman, Joseph and his wife Brenda, and their daughter Rachael with her new husband. The many friends and neighbor guests were seated with those they were most familiar with. The young people were seated at tables dedicated to their age group. I guess there were about four hundred guests in all. Jonathan, along with some other young people were just arriving as we were being seated at our table. Jonathan came over to our table and greeted all of us with hugs and kisses. He looked wonderful and seemed very happy.

Sara and Ari would have been so proud to see him at this moment. He had graduated with a degree in Business Accounting. He would be twenty two on his next birthday. His plans were to get his Masters degree with post graduate studies. He then would join the accounting firm that was owned by his uncle Joshua, and his grandfather Joseph.

At Jonathan's side was a very pretty young lady. He then introduced her to all at our table. Her name is Barbara Rosen. He then told us that she was his finance, and that she had just accepted his proposal to be his wife. I thought that this young lady had looked familiar when I first saw her, but when I heard her name, and looked at her more closely, I realized that she was one of the children from the orphanage whose name was on the list given to me by Sister Margaret. I then blurted out loudly, "The list", you are one of the children on the list. Jonathan smiled and said, "Yes grandfather, Barbara and I have kept in close touch over the years. Her adoptive parents live close by. We were soul mates at the orphanage, and I couldn't imagine going through life without her by my side. I love her very much." At that moment, Jonathan's great grandfather, Simon said in a very loud voice, "Mozzeltof", and all of us at our table raised our glasses in a toast to our future Mr. and Mrs. Jonathan Fenerman.

THE END